PARADISE

THE NARAVAN CHRONICLES 4

ISABO KELLY

PARADISE

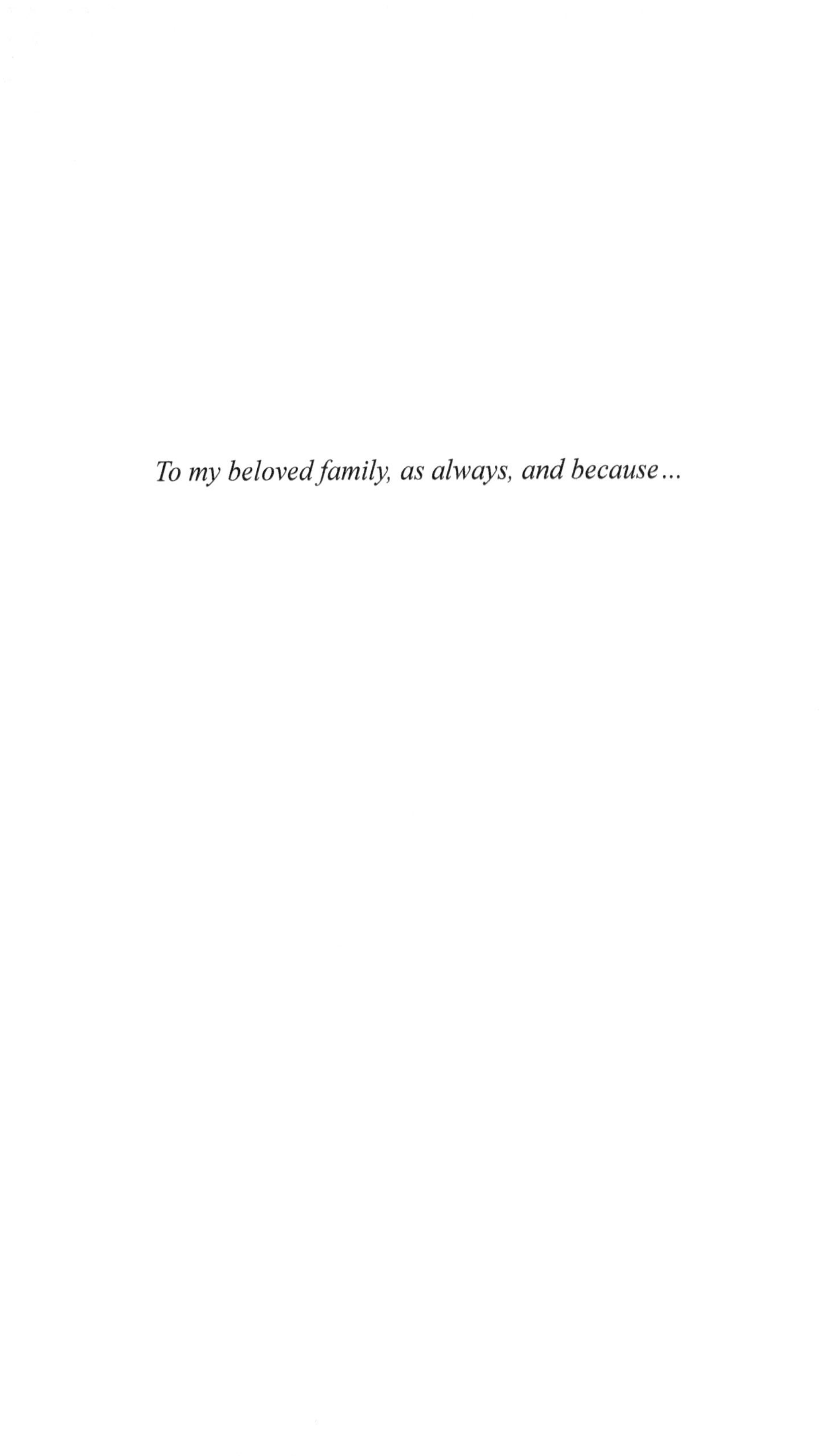

To my beloved family, as always, and because…

THE MINUTE LIEUTENANT BRAND STEPPED INTO HER OFFICE, Security Chief Meiling Trudeau knew she was about to receive news she didn't want to hear.

She sighed and leaned back in her chair. "Please tell me it's not the Binneans?"

They had two clans on FarMore Station at the same time, which was a recipe for disaster. Different clan members couldn't be anywhere near each other without trying to tear each other—and any poor bastard in the vicinity—to pieces. It was biology. It was also incredibly dangerous on a space station.

But since FarMore was an "open and neutral" station, mecca to both pleasure seekers and business people alike, Meiling was forced to contend with all kinds of potentially disastrous combinations of occupants on a regular basis. She worked hard to foresee the disasters and head them off.

She was successful more often than not.

"The Binneans are staying in their respective quadrants." Lieutenant Brand shifted from one foot to the other, not quite meeting Meiling's eyes.

That was so unusual it only deepened the level of dread tightening her stomach. "I know for a fact the Leeches aren't causing trouble." She hated having the mutants on station. She'd rather the entire Binnean populous descended on FarMore and held their impending war here than have to deal with Leeches. So she ensured they were watched closely.

"Correct, Chief."

Meiling waited a beat. When her lieutenant still didn't explain her presence, she said, "Brand, you need to spit it out, or I'm going to get very annoyed."

The lieutenant made a face, half cringe, half resignation. She held her hands out at her sides and said, "It's McClane."

Meiling scrubbed her hands over her face and tried hard not to groan. She'd warned Captain Varty not to let Duncan McClane back on station. He was a crook and a conman who couldn't resist pushing his luck and station law. As a result, he was one of the few people ever banned from FarMore. It didn't matter how rich he was now, how often he swore he'd gone straight, con-artists didn't change.

Meiling should know. She'd grown up surrounded by them.

She dropped her hands and stared at Brand. The recycled station air swirled around her, pleasantly scented and cool. It did nothing to stave off the heat of anxiety clawing at her muscles. "What's he done?"

"Cheated at the casino tables. Again. Not subtly this time, either."

Which meant he wanted Meiling to know. She'd been avoiding him since he'd returned to FarMore. The sono-fabitch knew this would force her hand.

"Which casino?" *Please not Paradise. Please not Paradise.*

"Paradise."

"Of course." She pressed her fingers into her temples to stave off a building headache.

Paradise was only the largest resort, with the most powerful owner, on FarMore. Ky Greven was the man responsible for having Duncan banned two years ago. The fact that Duncan was cheating him again could only mean impending disaster.

"Greven sent word that if you don't take care of McClane, he's gonna have his legs broken," Brand said.

Meiling was a little too tempted to let that happen. It went against everything she was supposed to be doing on this station, everything she'd made of her life here, but it would serve Duncan right for forcing her into this meeting.

"That's very restrained for Greven," she said. "Last time he nearly threw Duncan out an airlock."

Brand shrugged. "McClane's rich now and can actually repay debts. Greven can't get his money back from a corpse."

"True." Still…

How the hell was she going to face Duncan after all this time? She'd barely been able to resist him last time he was on station. Despite her best efforts, she had a weakness for sexy, clever conmen. Even after he'd betrayed her trust, Meiling had had trouble watching him leave, knowing he wouldn't be allowed back.

When he'd boarded the station two standard weeks ago, now one of the richest men in the galaxy, one look had been all it took to confirm she was still vulnerable to him. Which was why she'd assigned other people to deal with him. Why she'd been refusing his requests to meet.

Cowardly, but she saw it as self-preservation. Now Duncan had pushed the issue, and the only outcome would be more heartbreak.

She settled her hands on her desk and pushed to her feet, slowly, like a much older woman, body aching from the effort. She didn't want to do this. She didn't trust herself around him.

Though whether she was more afraid she'd take him to bed or kill him was a tossup.

"Come on, Lieutenant." She motioned to Brand. "I might need you to hold my blaster."

She ignored Brand's slight smirk as they left the office, heading down to Paradise—and Meiling's version of hell.

CHAPTER TWO

DUNCAN WATCHED THE CASINO ENTRANCE CLOSELY, EVEN AS he won another hand. Cheating at cards was so second nature, he'd fallen back into it easily despite a year and a half away from the gaming tables. He pressed a space on the green felt in front of him to move the holo-chips from the center of the table to his stack, then tapped the table edge for another game. The dealer cast a nervous glance to the huge human bouncer standing behind and to the left of Duncan. A moment later, another series of translucent cards flickered into an arch in front of him.

He smiled, only a little surprised they were still letting him play. Greven hadn't agreed to lose this much money on this ploy. Duncan had a feeling the casino owner had the table monitored, trying to figure out how Duncan *could* cheat when it should have been impossible. No one could count a holo-card deck—supposedly—and there were scanners on the tables to ensure no devices got added to enable cheating.

None of that had ever mattered to Duncan. He could always find a way. Seeking out the holes in security, finding the patterns in seemingly random arrays. It all came so naturally to him he rarely even thought about what he was doing.

Unfortunately, it was that unthinking propensity to cheat that had lost him the only woman in the universe he'd ever loved.

The universe had gifted him with a second chance, though, and he intended to take that chance. He just had to get Meiling to talk to him.

He spotted her the minute she stepped through the casino's entrance, flanked by one of her security people. She stared across the casino floor for a moment, as if letting her eyes adjust to the dim interior. Casino lighting was specifically designed to keep the people inside from noticing time— the rest of the station conformed to a standard day, with lights rising and falling to give the illusion of days and nights. The casinos wanted occupants to forget time was passing, to lose track of how long they'd been in the pit. They played longer if they didn't realize they'd been losing money for hours.

Duncan watched Meiling study her surroundings, assessing and scrutinizing without revealing her inner thoughts. She scanned the pit, her dark gaze taking in every detail before she turned, unerringly, to stare at him.

She didn't look happy.

He smiled anyway. Gods it was good to see her.

The crowds of revelers and gamblers cleared a path for her as she strode toward him. His heart thumped harder. She was tall, very tall—just shy of his 6'3"—and curved in all the right places. Her uniform, which was supposed to be relatively neutral with its gray and green color scheme and casual, almost plane-clothes lines, wasn't enough to disguise her lush shape. On duty, she had her long, straight black hair knotted in a severe bun at the base of her skull. The style highlighted the sexy tilt of her brown eyes and drew attention to the smoothness of her skin.

As she drew near, she set a hand to the blaster in her hip holster. The gesture sent a few slow-to-move tourists scattering out of her way. Duncan's smile widened, knowing that hand to her weapon was meant as a threat for him. Oh, he could see in her face she wanted to stun him. He also knew that reaction was because she cared more than she wanted to admit.

At least, he hoped she still did.

He tapped the table, sending two cards back while two fresh ones were dealt. He glanced down briefly before making his bet.

"All in," he said just as Meiling stopped next to him. He met and held her gaze as the dealer took his cards and called the game in Duncan's favor.

Meiling looked at the pile of credit chips he'd just won and closed her eyes. "Greven is going to shoot you out an airlock for sure this time," she muttered. When she looked up, her expression was neutral. "McClane," she said. "You promised the captain you wouldn't do this again."

He shrugged and turned in his seat to face her fully. The bouncer behind him shifted positions too, inching a step farther away but still hulking over Duncan.

"It's been too long, Chief," he greeted, watching her closely, hoping for a sign she'd missed him as much as he'd missed her.

"Who's responsible for that?" she countered, without emotion.

Damn. "Point. Can we talk?"

"No."

"I have an offer for you."

Her eyes narrowed to slits. "An *offer*?"

The disbelief in her voice was obvious. The threat in her expression would have made a lesser man step away from the conversation quickly.

Duncan loved it. She was the most spectacular woman he'd ever known. He just had to prove to her he was a changed man, the kind of man she could make a life with.

"Business," he said. "Promise."

"Your promises are worthless to me. You need to leave Paradise. Now."

"Not until you agree to meet with me."

"Not going to happen. There's no possible business you could have with me."

"I have a new security system."

"We have the best tech in the galaxy," she said matter-of-factly.

"True. Until now. My company's got a new design for a drop blast. It's species specific." He watched her eyebrows jump in surprise and knew he had her.

FarMore was a hotbed of potential disasters, not the least because it allowed anyone and everyone aboard all at once. If something truly disastrous happened and they had to activate a blanket drop blast, everyone within range—human, Binnean, Leech, droid, biologics, even Shifter (if one ever managed to make it past the detector rings and get off Narava)—would be shocked into unconsciousness. That included any security people in the thick of a fight.

Meiling hated the drop blast and refused to use it except as an absolute last resort. He was sure she'd get herself killed trying to avoid using the tech, especially to protect her people.

Which was why one of the very first things he'd put into motion after his "miraculous" discovery of the orphan planet was research into creating this new security system. The sheer quantity of merkesium he'd stumbled across—while on the run for his life from some people he really shouldn't have tried to con—was unprecedented. The ore was a vital component in most modern technology, especially the really good molecular scanning tech coming from Binnea. The discovery had made him an incredibly wealthy man and opened up tech options not possible before with so little merkesium available in the entire galaxy.

Almost as soon as he realized what he'd found, Duncan knew he finally had a way to win Meiling back. If he could create something that would help her do her job, help her protect her people and keep this station safe, she might just forgive him his idiotic past and give him another chance.

At least, that was his plan.

Her brow creased with her frown as she studied him. The bings, rings, and chink-chink-chink sounds of the casino filled the silence between them, though there was less noise in the immediate vicinity than usual, as if even the slot machines were trying to listen in on the confrontation. The serving droids handing out free drinks sashayed around the tables, quietly asking if anyone wanted a refill while avoiding the area directly surrounding Duncan's table.

"Take it to the captain," Meiling finally said. "Let her decide if she wants to risk the safety of the station to one of your…schemes."

"It's not a scheme. I don't do that anymore."

She glanced at the table and raised her brows again.

"Fine," he said with a shrug. "But this was just to get you here and you know it."

"Tell that to Greven," she muttered. Her mouth flattened into a line and she straightened her shoulders. "Talk to the captain."

"I have. And Greven. They both want your approval

first."

She blinked. "You talked to a casino owner about security tech?"

"He's willing to use Paradise as the test case for the new system…if you approve it."

"Ky Greven wants my approval?"

He understood her surprise. The casino owners and station security didn't always see eye-to-eye on what was best for the station as a whole. It wouldn't be unusual for Greven to try installing a new system without getting security's approval first—which was required under station regulations.

She frowned suddenly and glanced at the table. "If you and Greven are negotiating to work together—" Her jaw tightened and she rolled her eyes.

Duncan tried not to smile at her irritated grunt. He was a little surprised it had taken her this long to figure out Greven had been in on the ploy to get her here. Meiling had a sixth sense that let her recognize when she was being conned. Most of the time.

For a while, he'd thought maybe that was the reason he was so fascinated with her. He'd never been able to con her, at least not for long. She was a puzzle. A challenge. One he could spend the rest of his life trying to crack, and die content if he never did solve her mystery. When he'd realized he'd be happy even if he never figured her out, he knew he was in love.

Pressing her lips together into a tight line, Meiling glanced at the table again, then at the crowds trying to pretend they weren't listening to the conversation between one of the galaxy's richest men and the station's security chief. Everyone nearby quickly averted their gazes, but it was obvious this was as entertaining as anything happening at the tables or on the distant performance stage.

Meiling sighed, a noise half-annoyance, half-resignation. "Make an appointment. Bring the schematics." She put her hands on her hips and leveled him with her sternest look. "Pay Greven back all your winnings." She glanced at the bouncer still hovering behind him. "If he doesn't, you have my assurances security won't interfere with any…measures you deem appropriate."

Duncan raised his brows and glanced back at the bouncer. The man's grin was as scary as any Binnean's—and a Binnean grin could send even the bravest of humans running in terror.

Duncan turned back in time to see Meiling stalking away. The security person who'd accompanied her into the casino grinned at him before following the chief. Duncan chuckled. Well, at least one person wanted him to win this gamble he was taking with Meiling.

For a man who'd spent his life chancing his luck against the house, Duncan was coming to realize he'd never risked so much on one hand before. He just hoped the good luck that got him to this point held out a little bit longer.

CHAPTER THREE

Meiling remained seated as Duncan was shown into her office. She sat straight and kept her expression ruthlessly neutral. No small effort when he smiled at her in greeting. He had this way of grinning—all wicked and sexy, like he was contemplating things that would make a woman blush. She was a sucker for that expression. It called to all her most basic urges. Resisting smiling back was an act of will.

He settled in the chair across the desk and handed her a rolled up reader-sheet. "The schematics."

She set them aside, and he raised his brows.

"Not even a little curious?" he asked.

"Why are you here, Duncan?"

"For you."

She blinked. She hadn't been expecting such a straightforward answer. Worse was the fact that her bullshit meter didn't go off. Years of watching her parents con and lie had given her an excellent, innate lie detector. He wasn't lying.

"Why?" she asked. "Why me?"

A part of her kept thinking this *had* to be a scam. He was playing her. A long con. But she wasn't sure to what end. He didn't need money now—the one thing besides the rush that had always driven her parents—so what could he really want?

Another part of her hoped to hear he just thought she was worth the effort.

She hated that part. It reminded her of the little girl she'd been, desperate for attention from her lovingly neglectful parents, wanting them to prove she was worth enough to them to give up the cons and scams.

That had never happened. So she'd grown up, come into her own as a woman, and didn't look to others for acceptance anymore.

Ah, but a small part of her still wanted to be important to *someone*.

She realized she'd been waiting a bit too long for Duncan's answer and decided she really didn't want to know.

"Never mind," she said. "Has your tech system gone through tests with all species? Simulations or live tests? What are the secondary reactions? How long does the blast last?"

He smiled softly. "I wasn't avoiding your question, Mei. I was trying to figure out a way to tell you I've been in love with you since...probably since the first time I saw you.

Because I *know* you won't believe me. I knew when you finally agreed to go out with me two years ago it would be an uphill battle to convince you I loved you."

"I don't believe in love at first sight."

"I know you don't. But I do. And you're it."

Her heart thumped hard. She ignored it. "You're a con-artist, Duncan. What's the scam?"

"My only goal here is figuring out how to make you believe I'm not conning you."

"Not likely to happen."

"That's why I invented this security system."

She frowned.

"For you," he said, so easily. So matter-of-factly. "I know how you are about your people getting injured in a drop blast. I know you'll take a blaster shot before you'll approve the use of a drop. And I know one day that attitude will get you killed. Things are just too likely to go wrong on FarMore."

She rolled her eyes. He was right, and she wasn't too pleased to realize he knew her that well. "You don't have the tech knowledge to have developed a system like this." She waved a hand over the schematics.

He laughed. "Of course not. But I have the money and merkesium to make it happen." He waggled his eyebrows.

She felt her mouth ticking up in a grin and ruthlessly fought it down. Unfortunately, his cocky smile told her he'd seen her slip.

"Greven has confirmed he'll let Paradise function as a

test case," she said, getting back to business so she could avoid thinking about feelings. "You realize this could take a very long time. If there's no need to use the blast, it won't actually be tested in real life terms for months, maybe years."

"On FarMore?" He snorted. "You'll have an excuse to use it sooner rather than later. Especially with the brewing Binnean war everyone's whispering about."

She sighed. That was also, unfortunately, true.

"Besides, I'm here for the foreseeable future," he said. "I don't care how long this takes."

"Again, why?" she asked.

"Again. For you."

"You don't love me."

"Now who's trying to con whom?"

She let her gaze slip away from his and was embarrassed by her cowardice. Damn him, couldn't he just stay gone?

She looked at the rolled up screen beside her and pursed her lips. "Leave this with me," she said. "I'll go over it. Run it past my tech people. If they give the go-ahead, I'll approve limited use inside Paradise."

The triumphant gleam in his eyes scared her.

"One more thing," he said.

Her pulse jumped in a way that annoyed the hell out of her. "Now what?"

"Have a drink with me."

"No."

"Please."

She opened her mouth to say no again and just couldn't do it. The word would literally not pass her lips. She didn't want to have a drink with him because if she did, she might fall back into that longing for a deeper connection beyond friendship or casual sex.

He's a con. He's playing with you. She just wished she could see the angle. For the first time in her life, she seemed to be missing the scam and that drove her nuts.

"If it will make you feel better," he said, "you can grill me about anything you like."

She made a face. Then she realized she did want to hear his story—how he'd discovered the orphan planet that had made him rich. There were as many stories about his miraculous discovery as there were people telling the tale.

When she still hesitated, he said, "How about this? We go to Paradise and I show you how the system will be set up, where the activation panels will be located and disguised, how it will work in the casino? You can pretend it's a business outing."

Oh, he was good. Before the system was installed, she would have to approve everything. His excuse was perfect.

And her level of relief at having a good excuse to do something she really wanted to do was embarrassing.

"Fine," she said, pretending at reluctance she didn't feel. "After the techs have gone through the details. I'll send word when I'm ready."

"Fair enough."

He stood, suddenly enough that she blinked. She'd assumed she'd have to force him to go away.

She came around the desk to show him out, still a little worried about herself and how much she was looking forward to their "business meeting." She started to motion him toward the door and instead found herself in his arms.

For an instant, she was so stunned she didn't react. A terrible, dangerous lapse on her part. But the feel of his arms, strong around her, the heat of his body pressed against hers reminded her too clearly how much she'd missed having him this close. Her heart hammered. And despite all her screaming self-preservation instincts, she relaxed against him.

In her work boots, she was almost exactly his height, but he still managed to make her feel delicate and feminine and strong all at once. She'd never understood how he did that— made her feel vulnerable without feeling weak.

She had felt more herself with Duncan than she'd ever felt in her entire life. She used to think she could tell him anything and he'd never judge.

But that was because he couldn't judge, not with his history.

The reminder made her stiffen away from him.

He shook his head. "Almost had you there," he murmured. "For just a moment, you forgot you're not supposed to want me." He leaned close, putting his mouth just a breath from hers. "But you do want me, Mei. Despite everything. And I intend to use that against you."

"I can't decide if you're being very honest, or using the appearance of honesty to play me."

"Honest," he said. "With you, from now on, always honest."

"Then tell me the truth. Why are you going through all this trouble?"

"I *love* you, silly woman. I want you. I went straight for you."

"People like you don't give up the con, Duncan. Ever. Even if they love someone."

He tilted his head a little and she realized she'd revealed too much. Even Captain Varty, a woman Meiling considered a friend and confidant, didn't know about her parents. The captain only had very sketchy knowledge of Meiling's past.

That Meiling had just slipped with Duncan terrified her. Too easy. It was too easy to give him all of her. But she didn't want to do that. She didn't want to risk her heart on another con-artist who would always love the game more than her.

"You're wrong," he said, his deep voice quiet. "I'll prove it to you. I have all the time in the universe. I'm here for the long run, Mei. An honest businessman just looking to win back the woman he loves."

She shook her head, but he silenced her denial with a kiss. Just a gentle brush of lips but it was enough to send her pulse racing. Enough to ratchet up the internal argument between giving in and resisting him. When she should have pushed him away or, better yet, dropped him on his ass for his presumptuousness, she instead moved into him, gripping his waist, her fingers bunching in the material of his shirt. She pressed tight and returned his kiss because it felt natural and inevitable and perfect.

And yet so so wrong.

Which was probably why she wanted this so much. She might try to deny it, but she was her parents' daughter. Risks, chances, danger still held a little too much thrill for her. And Duncan McClane was all those things wrapped up into a sexy, delicious man.

He deepened the kiss, wrapping her even tighter, his arms flexing against her in a show of strength that thrilled her. He tasted of the sweet punch Paradise was known for—a combination of fruits designed to simulate tropical flavors from Earth. She rarely indulged in the drink and that was her excuse for continuing the kiss, for tasting him deeper, longer than she should have permitted.

He caressed one hand up her spine, settling his palm over the back of her neck, his fingers toying with the few strands of hair that had escaped her bun. She shivered. She was incredibly sensitive around her neck, and the sneaky bastard knew it. That should have been enough warning to make her push him away. It wasn't. Instead, she sighed into him and clenched him tighter.

She might have stayed in that haze of sensation for

longer if not for the ding of the comm-unit on her desk. The sound, bright and sunny, shocked her back to her surroundings.

She stepped away from Duncan fast, but he'd already dropped his hold. That was probably good because if he'd resisted at all, she would have used the excuse to flip him onto the floor. Heat crawled into her cheeks, the blush itself almost as embarrassing as the emotions that were making her blush. She stared at him a moment, then moved to her desk to answer the summons.

To her irritation, he didn't leave. He stood there, too close, and waited for her to acknowledge her assistant's reminder that she had another meeting. When she straightened, she forced herself not to step away from him, but her body was too aware of his, her skin tingling with heat and desire.

His breathing wasn't entirely steady yet either—a small victory. But the intensity in his eyes made it difficult to hold his gaze. She saw too much there she didn't want to see. Damn him, he wasn't holding anything back. How could she keep telling herself he was playing her when he wasn't actually hiding his feelings?

Or was he just that good an actor?

"I have been dreaming about doing that since I was kicked off FarMore," he said quietly. "You were with me when I crashed on the orphan planet, when I thought I was going to die. I wanted my last thoughts to be filled with memories of you. My last wish was one more chance to see you again. A chance to apologize for…disappointing you."

She swallowed hard. His confession hit home. Disappointed was the perfect word. Though he couldn't realize how much went into that disappointment.

He cupped her cheek. "I'm more grateful than you can imagine to have the reality of you again."

"You don't have me. One kiss doesn't mean—"

"I didn't mean that," he interrupted. "I meant, just being able to see you, hear you, watch you work… Being on the same station with you again is more than I ever thought I'd get. And it might have even been enough for me. Just to be in your presence." He smiled a little, the tilt of his lips self-deprecating. "If I hadn't kissed you just now, I *might* have been able to keep my distance. Not gonna happen now."

"And what if I ask you to stay away?" she said. "What if I say this isn't what I want anymore?"

"I'll insist on a chance first. To prove myself to you." He caressed a finger along her cheekbone then stroked that same finger down her neck.

She shivered in response. "And if I still ask you to leave me alone?"

"After a fair chance," he said, holding her gaze, "if you still don't want me, I'll let you go. I won't like it. But I will."

"Really? You could walk away?" She wasn't sure whether she believed him or not. Whether she hoped he was lying or telling the truth.

"I didn't say I'd walk away," he said. "I intend to stay on FarMore. If you refuse to see me anymore, I still want to know…to know you're safe and doing well. But I won't bother you or cause you trouble."

"What if I asked you to leave FarMore?" She was genuinely curious about this. Her parents could never leave behind a scam, even when it started to go wrong. Even when their only daughter begged them to drop the con and leave. Oh, he claimed this wasn't a con, and despite herself, she was starting to believe him. But would he be able to consider her wishes above his own? Ever?

He studied her for a long moment, and she didn't look away. She hadn't realized it when she asked, but this question was more important than anything else they'd discussed today, more important than the question appeared to be on the surface. And she wondered if he recognized that, too.

"If you ask me to leave, I'll leave," he said finally. "I wouldn't want to. And to be honest, I'd station someone I trust here to watch out for you. But if you really, truly wanted me off FarMore, I'd accept that and go."

Something cracked inside her, something she thought might be the wall around her heart. If this was a con, he was better than anyone she'd ever seen. If it wasn't…

She was in serious trouble.

She nodded her understanding without knowing what to say to his answer. Instead, she went back to focusing on work, a refuge against her tumultuous feelings. "I'll let you know when I'm ready to do the tour of Paradise."

"I'm looking forward to it." He dipped his head in a brief farewell and left.

Leaving Meiling torn between hope and resignation. And the sure knowledge she'd done the worst thing ever—fallen in love with a conman.

CHAPTER FOUR

Duncan worked hard at keeping his hands to himself as he led Meiling around the casino edges, laying out how his system needed to be installed, showing her the optimum locations for static activation panels. He'd waited an excruciating four days before she'd contacted him. Four days to replay that kiss in her office over and over.

Which meant he really hadn't slept much.

Her scent wafted to him as he moved a little closer to point out a strategic point on the casino floor. Jasmine and vanilla and Meiling. Subtle but powerfully addictive for him.

"Have you tested those boot inserts in real time?" she asked, her attention on the gaming pit and not on him.

"We have," he confirmed. The inserts protected the wearer from the effects of the blast. Most systems had something like it, but the cost of them usually meant only one person in an entire station had the inserts. He'd ensured enough were available for her entire security crew. "I wore a set myself during tests."

She faced him. "You experiment on yourself a lot?"

"Never. I'm risk averse."

The blatant lie made her laugh before she realized she wasn't supposed to be enjoying time with him and got serious again. He took the laugh as a small victory.

"Okay," she said as they stopped at a railing overlooking the card tables.

Their backs were to the nearest entertainment stage where a trio of human singers were pushing the boundaries of decency with their vocal range. Since that made hearing Meiling more difficult, he used the excuse to scoot close and talk into her ear. She didn't move away, and he took that as another victory.

"Does that mean we're good to install the system?" he asked.

"My techs assure me the schematics are sound, the design is good, and there are no hidden glitches." She angled her head to look him in the eyes. "At least not that they can find."

"Why would I risk the reputation of my very new company on a glitchy system?" he asked. "Especially one I had created just for you?"

She looked away but not before he saw something move through her eyes, an emotion he couldn't read but which made him nervous for some reason.

When she didn't answer, he said, "Come have a drink with me."

"I'm on duty."

"Pretend this is still business."

"It's too loud in here to talk business."

He put his mouth next to her ear, close enough he could almost taste her skin. "I'd say let's go back to your office but last time we were alone there you kissed me." His tone was teasing but husky from suppressed need.

She pulled away and glared at him. "You kissed me."

"You kissed back." He grinned and watched her cheeks color.

Her huff was so delicious he wanted to kiss her again. He had to keep reminding himself Meiling wasn't like the women he'd been used to in his previous life—the best thing about her as far as he was concerned. She was so totally herself. But it meant he couldn't push her the way he might someone else. He had to do this right if he had any hope of convincing her he really did love her.

He nudged her shoulder with his. "Come on. One drink. I'll stay on the opposite side of the table the whole time. I promise."

He motioned across the main floor to a lounge of booths with privacy screens to block out the floor noise—and hide any dirty deeds the vacationers wanted to indulge in. He half expected her to balk at going into one of those booths. Instead, she pushed back from the railing and led the way.

He just loved how he couldn't predict her. She was probably the only thing in his life he couldn't predict. Even the chaos that followed him was predictable—he pushed his luck (and knew he was doing it), got himself into trouble with dangerous people, and they tried to break his legs. Or shoot him out an airlock. Or some variation on that.

Meiling never did what he expected.

She slid into a booth near the back of the lounge, away from any other patrons and facing the main floor. They waited on the droid-server to produce drinks—two Paradise punches without the Binnean brandy shot—then he activated the shield to block out the sounds around them. He considered triggering the full privacy mode which made the shield opaque but decided she'd trust him more if he left their booth visible to the rest of the casino.

She smiled a little into her glass. "Smart," she murmured.

"Always have been," he said.

That comment made her look at him with her chin back and her brows raised.

He laughed. "Okay. Maybe lucky is a better word."

"Lucky?" There was disbelief in her tone then she frowned a little and shrugged. "Actually, you are exceptionally lucky, aren't you? Even to still be alive is an accomplishment."

He raised his glass in a silent salute before taking a sip of the coconut and pineapple flavored punch. This version was a great combination of tart and sweet without the burn of alcohol. He'd grown a little addicted to the stuff since arriving. But as he watched Meiling sip more of it, he decided what he really wanted was to taste it on her.

He blinked and shook his head when she narrowed her eyes.

"You're thinking things you shouldn't be, aren't you?" she asked.

"Who says I shouldn't be thinking them?"

"One kiss does not mean I'm going to start seeing you again." But her expression was less determined than her words. She lifted the tall, frosted glass. "I don't really drink this often. I keep forgetting how good it is."

He smiled. "I was just thinking how addictive it was."

"That's what you were thinking?"

"Part of what I was thinking," he said.

"Do I want to know the rest?" she asked.

"Only if you want me to break my promise about staying on this side of the booth."

"No," she said, very firmly. "I don't." She took another sip then set her glass aside. "Everyone thinks your system is great. The captain, my techs, Greven. I've met with him, too. Did he tell you?"

Duncan nodded.

"So why do I still think it's a bad idea?" she asked.

"Good question," he said. "Why do you doubt everyone

else?" He tilted his head. "Just because I'm the one selling it, right? I know you don't trust me anymore, but why would I give you and your people access to all the data if I were scamming you?"

"It's the best kind of scam—when the mark thinks they have all the information because the con *seems* to offer full transparency."

He considered her a moment before saying, "Can I ask you something?"

She shrugged.

"This internal lie-detector you have… How did you develop it?" He'd never asked before, mainly because the first time they were together he was afraid to draw her attention to the topic. Convincing the head of security to get involved with a known conman had been tough enough, without reminding her of the subject.

She looked away. "It happened a long time ago. I don't talk about it."

"How about a story trade?" he offered.

She raised her brows. "Anything?"

"Anything."

A slightly devious expression crossed through her brown eyes, and for a moment he wondered if he should be worried.

But the deviousness shifted to thoughtfulness and she finally said, "I want the *real* story of how you found the orphan planet. Not the company hype. The truth."

"It's much less heroic than the public tales," he warned.

"I already guessed that."

"Hey." He tried to be offended but her slight smile was too charming. It was so nice to have her teasing him again that he decided to ignore her—unfortunately accurate—assessment of his heroism.

He leaned back in his seat and shrugged. "As you know, in my previous life I was a little…reckless."

She snorted agreement. "Has anything changed?"

"Some things. I've refocused my more reckless behavior."

"On what?"

"You."

She blinked, before waving his comment away. "Back to your previous unlawful days."

He waited a beat then continued. "After I got kicked off FarMore, I went through a self-destructive period."

"You mean all the scamming, cheating, and conning before *wasn't* self-destructive?"

"No. That was just skill and habit. I liked the rush of pushing the limits, but I never actually *tried* to get into trouble. Chaos just follows me around."

"Maybe if you didn't tempt chaos to dance, he'd leave you alone."

He shrugged. "Maybe. But I've had disasters rise up around me when all I was doing was having a drink. I decided early on it was easier to start the fight than to be an innocent bystander sucked up into the middle of things."

"That makes no sense, you know?" she said.

"It did at the time. At any rate, when I lost you, I went out of my way to get into trouble. Did a lot of things I'm not particularly proud of."

When he paused, she waved a hand for him to continue. "Like?"

"Like," he said with a sigh, "conning a group of religious missionaries out of their ship and leaving them stranded on Narava."

"Duncan."

He deserved her scolding tone. "I know. I told you. I'm not proud of what I did. I was in the Docks, and I'd gambled a lot more than I could possibly repay at one of the mob-owned gaming hells."

She closed her eyes briefly and he could only guess what she was thinking. She was originally from Narava. She knew what kind of place the Docks was and what happened to people who crossed the mob families that ran the haven for sin and debauchery.

"Yeah, I know," he said again. "Sounds pretty suicidal. I didn't think about it at the time. I wasn't consciously trying to get killed, but looking back on it, I suspect a part of me was courting death as much as chaos."

"Is that why you stole the missionaries' ship?" she asked.

"Needed to get off planet fast. They already had a clearance code, and I was desperate." He shifted a little in his seat. "I figured someone in Capital would help them out, get them a new ship. Besides, there are worse places to be stranded than Narava—so long as you're not a Shifter."

"What happened after you got off-planet?" she asked.

"The mobmen weren't far behind me. I went through a series of random jumps—"

"Duncan!" she said in a near screech. "You didn't?"

He raised his hands. "I knew at the time it was stupid. But I was desperate to get away. I didn't even know how much I wanted to live until I started running. I did try to ensure I was jumping into empty space, but…"

Jumping without precise coordinates was beyond reckless. You just never knew if you might jump into a star or the interior of a passing asteroid. Space was a lot more crowded with random bits of matter than most humans had suspected before they took to the stars.

She sighed. "Did you jump into the orphan?"

"Near to it, yes. Got lucky."

She groaned at the word and he smiled a little before continuing.

"I popped up close enough that the ship felt the gravity tug," he said.

"Geezus," she breathed.

He tilted his head in a slight shrug. "If not for that tug, I might have missed the planet. I was revving up to jump again, but, well, the missionaries' ship wasn't up to all that quick movement. The drive gave out on me. I had just enough axillary power to get to the little ball of rock, so that's where I went, hoping the entire time the mobmen wouldn't track me there. At a guess, I figured they were maybe two jumps behind me."

"How were they tracking you through jumps?" she asked.

"After I landed, I searched the ship. Turns out the missionaries had tagged it in case someone tried to steal it. They must have given the tracking signature to the Naravan Guard. Maybe even the mobmen themselves."

She dropped her chin. "You think the missionaries would send gangsters after you? Not very religious."

"I conned them. I wouldn't be surprised."

She leaned forward, settling her forearms on the table between them. "If the ship was tagged, why didn't the mobmen find you on the orphan?"

"Turns out I broke more than the drive with all the random jumps. Most of the ship's systems—including the tracker—got blown out."

"So you were stranded? On a small planet roaming randomly through space?" She shook her head. "How did you get out of that?"

He chuckled. "I am the luckiest bastard in the entire galaxy."

"Yes. You are," she said, very seriously. "What happened?"

"There was some gravity but obviously no atmosphere,"

he said, "so I suited up and went exploring. Fortunately, the missionaries had just restocked. I had food and water to last a few weeks. Some equipment and parts to possibly repair the ship. And a little remaining drive fuel gel. I was out of all the trade routes, so I couldn't hope for rescue." He winced. "And I was a little afraid of attracting the mobmen if I sent out an SOS signal anyway."

"And you stumbled across the largest vein of merkesium, just randomly?"

Her expression showed the same disbelief he'd felt at the time.

"Basically," he said, raising his hands palms up, a gesture of surrender. "The orphan is covered in the stuff. I could see thick lines of it inside some of the meteor craters pocking the planet's surface. Obviously, I could only explore so far from my ship, so there was this whole huge planet I couldn't get to. But when I realized what I was seeing, I knew even one of those veins would make me wealthy, and the crater nearest the ship had about seven."

She let out a low whistle. Then she frowned. "Little use to you if you couldn't get away."

"Yeah, that was a problem," he said. "Discovering the biggest score of my life, just as I'm about to die." He leaned forward and rested his arms on the table. The position mirrored hers and put them that much closer to each other, but she didn't seem to notice. "I decided to make some plans," he continued. "The first of which was to officially register my claim for the planet."

Space exploration was governed by a form of law similar to old Earth's maritime law, giving rights to those who discovered something—so long as they claimed it through the correct channels. A new planet could be claimed by its finder by official registration. You just had to get the registration recognized fast.

"Obviously," he said, "the claim wouldn't make it back to the trade planets until I returned to known space, but it wasn't likely anyone else would stumble across my planet and try to claim it before I could. I just wanted it set up and ready to transmit as soon as possible."

"Fair enough given what you'd discovered," she said. "But again, pointless if you couldn't get off the wanderer."

He nodded. "I spent the next three standard weeks repairing the ship's systems as best I could with what was aboard. I've got enough tech knowledge to do a fair job. I reserved the fuel I had left—just enough for one good jump —by keeping the life support on the ship at its absolute minimum. Cold as all hell, but since I stole a ship from missionaries, I figured I deserved that."

"You did."

He grinned at that. "In the end, I got things fixed and took my chance."

He tried to act casually about the danger, but at the time, he'd been terrified. If his efforts had failed, if he'd made a mistake in the repairs, he might have died a slow, extremely uncomfortable death in deep space with no hope of anyone ever stumbling across him. He still had the occasional nightmare about that time. In the nightmares, the ship turned into a floating rock not unlike the wandering planet, and he felt his lungs seizing up as the life supports failed. He always woke in a sweat, gasping for air, desperate to replace oxygen he hadn't actually been denied.

Despite his efforts to hide the residual fear he still experienced, he must have shown Meiling something because she reached across the table and squeezed his hand, a move that was both shocking and comforting all at once. He turned his hand over to grip hers, holding her for a few moments before allowing her to pull away.

He flexed his fingers, his palm warm and tingling from their contact. He forced a smile. "As I said, I'm the luckiest bastard in the galaxy." He met her gaze. "I got through it because of you."

She straightened. "Me? What did I have to do with anything?"

"I thought of you the entire time. When I wanted to give in to what most would consider the inevitable, I focused on my memories of you and went back to engine repairs. I wanted to see you again, more than I wanted anything else. Even the wealth I knew would come from my accidental discovery. I just wanted to see you again."

She shook her head. "Duncan."

His name sighed out of her and made his heart thump hard. If he hadn't promised to stay on his own side of the booth, he'd have gone to her then, pulled her into his arms and kissed her even with the entire casino watching.

He didn't, but only because he'd promised her.

<h1 style="text-align:center">CHAPTER FIVE</h1>

WHEN SHE SEEMED AT A LOSS FOR SOMETHING ELSE TO SAY, Duncan decided they'd had enough of his sorry story. He waved a hand in the air and said, "So there's the 'heroic' tale. Pretty pathetic really. But it's the truth. I've become richer than most people can even imagine because I'm an idiot who also happens to be extremely lucky."

Meiling glanced away and said, "You seem to be doing something positive with your newfound wealth. Everyone has only good things to say about the way you run your business."

"I figured I owed that for all my luck. I could have sold my interest and still been exceptionally wealthy. But I wanted to make sure workers were taken care of and the ore only went to the reputable refineries." He smiled crookedly. "Penitence for stealing a missionaries' ship."

She chuckled.

"Enough of this," he said. "It's too ridiculous a story."

She opened her mouth to say something more, then shrugged. "Fine."

"Your turn," he urged.

With a sigh, she let her gaze run over the lounge and, beyond it, the casino floor. "I don't really tell anyone about my parents. Even the captain doesn't…" She pulled in a deep breath. "They were con-artists, too." She faced him suddenly, looking him right in the eyes.

"Ah." That's how she could spot a con so easily.

"Exactly. I was raised by two people who lied and cheated for a living. They were mostly pretty good at it, but it's not a stable existence for a child. We were always on the run, a few steps ahead of the people they'd cheated. I just wanted a home in one place and some friends my age. They couldn't give up the rush and high of the game." She shrugged. "Not much more to it."

"Hey, we agreed on truth. You're leaving something significant out." She wasn't the only one who could spot a lie.

She grunted. "Their last big scam before I finally left involved selling a fake security system to one of the food processing plants on Narava. My parents assumed the useless tech they were hocking would just not work once it was installed." She glanced down at the table. "They were wrong. They'd been dealing with people who were skilled enough to make something that sort of worked. So when it finally did fail, it failed explosively. Several people died."

He closed his eyes and groaned. And here he was, selling her a security system.

"I promise you," he said, opening his eyes to meet hers, "I promise you, my tech will *not* do that. I have a lot of misdeeds I have to atone for, and some luck I have to justify. I would never risk your life or the lives of the people on this station."

She shook her head. "I actually do know that. I want to doubt what I 'know' because I watched my parents shill bad tech with excellent schematics and clever talk. But you've shown us everything. Greven's people are good with your hardware. So are mine. And I know since discovering the orphan, you've only done good work."

"But?" he prompted.

"But...people don't change. I'm waiting for the old you to reappear. I'm waiting for you to go back to the rush."

"I love you more than the rush," he said bluntly, not even blinking when she met his gaze. "I'm not going back to what I was."

"Even if I refuse to take you back?"

"Even if. Even if you send me off FarMore. Even if I have to give you up forever. I intend to be a man worthy of you, even if I can't have you. You saved my life."

She waved that away. "I didn't do anything for you. You saved yourself."

"I survived for you."

"I don't know what to say to that, Duncan."

"You don't have to say anything. It's a simple truth. And I told you I'd be honest with you from now on. So here's me being honest. My tech is good. My heart is yours. And I intend to live as an honest businessman from now on, to honor you."

A slight hint of that mischievousness glinted in her eyes again. "What if I was only attracted to you because you were a thief? You ever consider I might think an honest businessman is boring?"

He laughed. "This is why I love you. You keep me on my toes." He was about to say more, but her expression shifted suddenly, going serious and intent as she gazed out into the casino.

"What's wrong?" he asked, following her gaze. "Ah hell."

They'd seen the t'Kalb clan Binneans currently in Paradise earlier, during their tour of the place. He knew those Binneans hadn't left yet—there was no way to miss a group of over-large, hair-covered Binneans moving through the crowd. He also knew the four standing at the entrance to Paradise were not t'Kalb clan. The tan, gold, and rust color of their fur and the more grey-green eye color marked the newcomers as members of t'Pree clan.

The entire casino floor wasn't large enough to prevent the

biological reaction that sent different clans of Binneans into a killing rage around other clans.

Which meant serious trouble was about to erupt.

"Ah hell," he said again.

MEILING WANTED to curse but she didn't have time. She launched out of the booth, pushing through the privacy shield without deactivating it—which sent a tingling shock of discomfort through her nerves, but not enough to slow her down.

She arrowed through the crowd, heading right for the four Binneans hovering at the casino entrance. She was aware of Duncan following her. From her peripheral vision, she spotted some of Paradise's bouncers and private security also making their way toward the entrance while others moved back toward the last place she'd seen the t'Kalb Binneans.

She pulled out her comm-link and sent the emergency message to everyone on duty, the tracking chip on the link letting them know the trouble was in Paradise.

She reached the t'Pree Binneans first and placed herself squarely in front of them before they could step any farther into the casino.

"No," she said with all the command she'd spent years developing. "You know the rules. This is outside your quadrant."

"The casinos in our quadrant are inferior to Paradise," one of the two larger Binneans said, stepping up close.

She was as tall as he was, but he was easily three times her width and all of it was rippling muscle under his thick layers of fur. His long nose dipped close to the firm line of his mouth, adding an element of threat to his expression without his actually having to glower or frown.

"The casinos in your quadrant are excellent," she said without so much as leaning back. "And if you insist on breaking the required separation between yourself and t'Kalb, I will not hesitate to throw you off this station—never to return. I will not have clan fighting aboard FarMore." She glanced down at the obvious blaster nestled in the spokesman's forearm holster. "If you were just here to gamble, you wouldn't need to be armed."

"You're armed," he said, and grinned that absolutely terrifying Binnean smile that was all teeth and felt like a threat even when it was meant to be humor.

In this case, Meiling was positive the grin was an actual threat. She didn't even blink, despite the fact that her stomach tightened in response to the danger. "I'm in charge," she said, letting her voice drop to a deeper octave, quiet and deadly. "My station. My rules."

The Binnean opened his mouth to say more but before he could, Duncan stepped up next to her.

"Friends!" he said, his tone overly loud and enthusiastic. "It's obvious to me you're just on FarMore for a good time and to do a little business. I'm well versed in both." He held his hand up, palm out, to exchange a Binnean greeting. "I'm Duncan. Duncan McClane."

The spokesman frowned at him until Duncan said his name. Suddenly, the Binnean's expression changed. The hulking threat went out of his stance and he faced Duncan fully. He put his fist gently against Duncan's palm, returning the greeting. "You're the one with all the merkesium," the Binnean said.

"And your clan is in the middle of some very innovative research. I understand you could use a better supply of merkesium."

The spokesperson looked over his shoulder at his fellow clan members, then back at Duncan. "We could."

"Excellent! How about we go have a drink and discuss it. I'm sure we can come to a mutually profitable arrangement. Shall we adjourn to Pan's Palace? I understand they have a superior brandy on hand." Duncan motioned the four huge beings back toward the station corridors, smiling his most charming smile.

As the Binneans proceeded him out the door, he glanced back at Meiling and winked. "I'll be in touch."

Meiling blinked a few times, wondering what had just happened.

Seeing Duncan *prevent* a fight rather than start one, though, was…illuminating. A warm tingling swirled in her stomach, a rush of pleasure and giddiness she knew meant trouble.

CHAPTER SIX

Thanks to the near disaster, Ky Greven, Captain Varty, and Meiling all got behind rushing the installation of Duncan's new drop blast system. Meiling also made sure the entire station knew what was being installed and what it could do.

She was only a little surprised Duncan's people got the system set up as quickly as they did, and within a week, they were finalizing the tests and declaring the installation a success. If nothing went wrong over the next two standard months—the time it had taken for her parents' dodgy security tech to explode all those years ago—Meiling agreed to allow station-wide installation, with the enthusiastic support of the captain.

The process took so much of Duncan's time, Meiling barely saw him that week, a fact that was both relief and disappointment. She kept hearing his words, "I love you."

The way he batted that phrase around so freely and easily, as if they'd been lovers for years.

For all her parents had loved her, they hadn't been free with the words. She just wasn't used to hearing someone say them, not in a serious way. She had no experience saying them either. And she spent the week worrying she would never be able to say those three little words, to anyone. She could feel love. She suspected she was in love with Duncan. But to say it out loud...

After the system was up and running, Meiling expected Duncan to hunt her down. She even found herself watching her comm-link for messages from him. Yet that week passed with no word. When another standard week passed, and the system at Paradise continued to function without any glitches, she justified checking up on Duncan by convincing herself his silence might mean he was up to no good.

What she discovered was that he'd set up a very profitable trade with t'Pree clan, a deal which made the t'Pree so happy they departed FarMore without causing any trouble. They even sent one of their tek'la—a rare Binnean who didn't have the violent biological reaction to other clans and so could negotiate between clans without issue—to discuss a new manufacturing contract with the t'Kalb still on the station.

Somehow, it looked like Duncan had arranged a peace between two clans that had been on the verge of conflict.

Meiling had no idea how he'd managed it, but the rumors were that the looming threat of a Binnean war had eased somewhat. Things progressed so peacefully, the captain agreed to allow two other clans on station even while the t'Kalb were still aboard because they all claimed an interest in the new trade agreements. And they paid a substantial fee to conduct the negotiations on FarMore. The captain gave Duncan all the credit for the peace.

Everything Meiling heard about the situation surprised and baffled her. Duncan orchestrating a *peace*? The man he'd been before would have *started* a war—even if he didn't mean to.

His actions went a long way toward confirming that he'd gone straight. So much so, she was looking forward to seeing him again rather than dreading it. She was starting to think they could have something. That maybe, just maybe she could believe him when he said he loved her and he'd changed.

But then another week passed in silence. When a fourth week went by and she hadn't heard a word from him, all her good thoughts soured, leaving her feeling like an idiot. She'd allowed herself to fall for him again, and all the while he was playing some kind of game.

She couldn't figure out what game it was, and that was as irritating as anything else. She had no idea why anyone would claim to be in love with someone and then never try to see them. But it was obvious his feeling weren't as overpowering as he'd made her believe or he would never have stayed away so long.

Okay, fine, she wasn't going out of her way to contact him either. But she was the injured party here. Wasn't it up to him to prove his sincerity to her?

Irritation and hurt got her pride up. If he didn't want to see her, fine. She hadn't wanted to see him again anyway.

Two days after deciding she was done with Duncan, she was at her desk taking care of a budget issue, trying not to think about Duncan or her hurt feelings, when her comm-link buzzed. She picked it up just as the emergency beacon on the link went off, the tracker chip centered squarely on Paradise.

Sonofabitch. She was out the door in a blink, strapping on her weapons holster. As she jogged through the station corridors to the lift that would take her to Paradise, she tried buzzing Lieutenant Brand as she was supposed to be on duty in that quadrant. She didn't get an answer until she was out of the lift and running toward the casino.

"Chief." Brand's voice was loud against a cacophony of screams and blaster fire.

"I'm almost there. Report."

"Binnean fight, all three clans showed up at the same time. Don't know why yet. Blaster fire. Outer station shields holding."

Meiling had never been so grateful for FarMore's superior security tech. "Civilian casualties?" She was close enough now she could hear the screams and shouts without the comm-link. She put the link back into its place on the shoulder of her uniform and pulled her blaster.

"Can't tell," Brand answered. "We're evacuating now."

Meiling met the crowd of fleeing people then, nearly getting mowed under by the swarm. She motioned them past her as she made her way toward the casino entrance. Despite her hesitance, and her worry it wouldn't actually work, this was exactly what Duncan's new system was for. It was time to give it a real world test.

"You have your inserts?" she shouted into the link. "Activate the drop blast."

"We're being held down," Brand shouted back. "Can't get to the nearest panel."

"Where the hell is Greven?" Meiling reached the casino entrance, taking cover just outside the door as more civilians stumbled past. She risked a glance inside, squinting to see through the smoke, flash of blaster fire, and flickering uneven lighting which was obviously damaged in the fight.

"Got caught at the back of the casino with his men," Brand answered.

Great. Meiling knew she'd never hear the end of it once she and Greven met about this mess. She'd refused to allow him a portable activation link because, frankly, she didn't trust him to use it only when absolutely necessary. He was going to use this disaster against her. Though she had a few questions for him, too. Like how the hell had three different clans of Binneans who were supposedly getting along all ended up in the same damned casino. If he'd orchestrated this…

She pulled in a deep breath and dove through the entrance to the nearest overturned gaming table, taking cover behind its bulk. A blaster shot sizzled the electronics on the underside of the table, opposite her position but creating so much heat she winced.

"I'm inside," she shouted to Brand as she pulled her link from its holder and studied the positions of her people throughout the casino. Most of them had formed a line to cover the fleeing civilians. It put them dangerously close to the heart of the fight and, unfortunately, too far away from any of the drop blast panels. Only a handful of people had the codes, at any rate. Even if someone other than Brand had been close enough, they wouldn't have been able to activate it. And Brand was on the opposite side of the huge gaming floor.

Meiling took advantage of a lull in the shots and peaked around her cover. "I'm near the panel at the center of the floor," she told Brand. "Give me some covering fire so I can reach it."

Another volley of shots sizzled through the air, fast and heavy, toward the middle of the fight, though some arched over her toward another area of fighting to the rear and left of her. She charged toward the panel, keeping low and ducking behind cover when she could.

She reached the pedestal designed to look like part of the

casino's tropical décor without getting hit, but a few shots came near enough to singe her hair. She rose to her knees, putting her face level with the holo plant on top of the pedestal. A bolt of blaster fire punched the ground so close she had to duck again, covering her head and hoping against hope she wouldn't get hit.

Before she could rise enough to fire back, the sound of a blaster shot zinged just above her head. She looked up to see Duncan crouching next to her, firing into the melee, covering her.

"Thanks," she said, loud enough for him to hear over the noise. She pushed up to her knees again and deactivated the holo-palm fronds on top of the pedestal. Then she placed her hand against the panel lock and positioned her face in front of the retinal scanner. The cover whooshed open, revealing the keypad.

"You wearing inserts?" she asked.

"No. Won't matter." He fired again, then glanced at her. "Trust me."

She swallowed and punched in the code to activate the drop blast, using the Binnean species specific sequence. She cringed a little, anticipating the jolt even as she moved to her feet so her inserts would take the blast and keep her conscious if anything went wrong. Then she hit the activate command sequence.

A tremor shook the floor and she felt a tingling of energy along her nerves, like lightning, or passing through a privacy screen without deactivating it. Nothing painful, nothing to knock her out, but an obvious shock of energy being released.

A few screams echoed through the casino as the blaster fire stopped abruptly, and the Binneans she could see from her position dropped to the ground in large, hairy heaps. For several long moments, silence echoed, making her ears ring after all the noise.

Very slowly she rose, scanning the floor, taking in the residual chaos. A few human bodies were scattered about, but more had survived. They rose to their feet, looking around like the confused survivors of a crash.

Meiling spotted the closest of her security people. "Get the rest of the humans out of here," she ordered. "Someone find me Greven. You two—" she motioned to two more of her people, "—get all the Binneans restrained before they wake up. Take them to holding. But for gods' sake be sure to put each clan on a different level."

One of the two men actually barked a laugh at that comment, a sound more strained than amused.

Once she was sure her people were cleaning up the mess, she turned to face Duncan. "What are you doing here?"

"I was on my way here to talk to Greven when I heard the noise. I saw you go in and followed."

"Well that was a dumb ass thing to do. You could have been hurt."

He scowled. "So could you. You think I'd stand back while you charged into that chaos on your own?"

"I wasn't on my own. I had half the security team here." She pointed over her shoulder toward her crew.

He put his face in hers, his scowl deepening. "And against pheromone-crazed Binneans that's worth exactly squat."

Her voice rose as she said, "Hey, you're the reason we've got three clans on station at once."

"You think this is my fault?" His voice rose right along with hers.

"No," she shouted. "I'm just upset and I need to yell at someone."

"Fine," he shouted back. "Yell at me all you like then."

"Thank you," she barked. "Are you hurt?"

"No. Are you?"

"No. Why haven't you called me?" She growled this last with more anger than even her previous yelling. Her adrenaline was still pumping in the aftermath of the fight, and she was too wound up to hold back.

His scowl softened into a very slight smile. "I've been waiting."

"What the hell for?"

Before he could answer, Brand trotted up to her. "Everything's under control now, Chief. Greven is still barking orders to his people to secure the money." She rolled her eyes. "Said he'd meet with you as soon as he was sure the place wouldn't be robbed in the aftermath."

Meiling snarled a little. "Fine. Tell him to come to my office once he's got things settled. In the meantime, I want you to question the clans as soon as they come to. What the hell were they all doing here?"

Brand nodded and trotted off to finish the clean-up.

Meiling turned her attention back to Duncan. "You didn't have anything to do with this, did you? Please tell me you didn't organize this to prove the system would work?"

"Of course not."

He looked so offended and outraged she believed him. *No one* was that good an actor.

"Fine," she said. "Do you suppose Greven arranged it?"

Duncan looked out over the now wrecked casino floor. "I think if he'd arranged this, he would have positioned himself near a drop blast panel before the fight got started. Even he wouldn't want this much damage. He's gonna have to shut Paradise down for a week or more to get things cleaned up and working again."

She sighed, agreeing with his assessment.

"But…"

At his hesitance, she gave him the side-eye. "But what?"

"I overheard something a few hours ago that I wasn't supposed to hear."

"Eavesdropping?" she asked.

He shrugged, unrepentant. "I've discovered it's better to

have more information than less." He grinned briefly before turning serious again. "One of the two newest clans on station has a vested interest in making sure a trade agreement doesn't happen between t'Kalb and t'Pree. They aren't really here to deal. They're here to make sure the fighting continues."

"How if only t'Pree's tek-la is still on station? How could this fight damage the relationship between t'Kalb and t'Pree? And why have the fight here at Paradise?"

"The t'Pree tek-la has been meeting with t'Kalb here," he said.

Ah. She closed her eyes as the realization hit. If the t'Pree tek-la was killed in a fight t'Kalb was involved in, t'Kalb would take the blame for it and the peace would break down. Again.

"Damn it." She glanced around for Brand, didn't see her, so buzzed her on the comm-link. When Brand answered, she said, "Do we know if the t'Pree tek-la was here and if she survived the fight?"

"Not yet, Chief. Give me a second to check."

While Meiling waited, she asked Duncan, "Why didn't you tell me as soon as you heard this?"

"I was trying to contact you on your link while I made my way here to warn Greven, but I couldn't get through. I intended to hunt you down in your office right after meeting Greven." He winced a little. "I thought maybe you were avoiding me and had put a block on my calls."

She made a face. Actually, she hadn't thought to do that, but it did sound like something she might consider doing in a snit. "I was ignoring other comm-link pings while I was on with Brand." She gestured to the wreckage around them.

"I figured that out when I got here."

Another minute passed in silence as Meiling waited anxiously for Brand to get back to her. If the tek-la had been killed on FarMore, the station could get pulled into the Binnean conflict. Which would be a disaster on more levels than Meiling wanted to consider.

When Brand finally buzzed her, she answered with a harsh, "Well?"

"She's alive, Chief," Brand said, sounding as relieved as Meiling felt. "She was in Paradise during the fight and was put in holding with the t'Kalb. We're having her moved to medical."

"Was she injured?"

"No. Just thought we should move her to a more neutral location while she recovers from the drop blast."

"Good. When she comes to, tell her I need to talk with her in private." Meiling didn't think she'd be able to prevent any Binnean wars, but she was definitely going to make sure they didn't start on *her* station.

As she disconnected with Brand, she met Duncan's gaze again. He was watching her, his expression serious but relaxed now that they knew the tek-la was safe. The events of the last hour settled into the back of her mind, something she'd get cleaned up, and the station would return to normal. Just another day on FarMore.

But wars aside, she still had one remaining nagging question for Duncan. One she needed answered. "Why haven't you been in touch with me before this?"

He tilted his head and shrugged. "I did a little research and found out the fake security system your parents used for their scam lasted seven standard weeks before it malfunctioned. I wanted to wait out that period, so you could be sure *my* system was legitimate."

She opened her mouth to respond but couldn't find words. She *had* been waiting out that same period of time, counting the days, watching for something to go wrong. She hadn't thought about it consciously since setting the test period at two standard months, but in the back of her mind she'd been tracking the weeks—and not just because she hadn't heard from Duncan.

He cupped her cheek. She was so stunned she didn't think to step away, even though her people were still scattered around the casino.

"Meiling," he said quietly, "I want you to trust me, to *know* I won't con you. Or anyone else for that matter. Whatever it takes to do that, I will."

"Your system worked," she said. "Exactly the way you claimed it would. When I really needed it to."

"Told you so," he said with a half-smile. "I put a lot of money into developing this system."

She smiled, then chuckled.

"Does that mean you forgive me for not calling?" He stepped closer so their bodies were touching, and moved his hand from her cheek to the back of her neck, his fingers brushing against the sensitive skin there. "Does this mean you might consider…trusting me?"

"It's a hell of a start," she said. "A hell of a good start."

"Do you believe I love you now?"

She set her forehead to his. "Terrifyingly, yes. Yes, I do."

"Good."

"Even more terrifyingly, I might just… You know. Back."

He laughed. "Can't say it yet?"

She cringed. "Can you wait on that too? The words… They might take me a little more time."

He lifted her chin up so she had to look him in the eyes. "I'd wait the rest of my life for you, Meiling. Just knowing how you feel is enough."

"I will say the words eventually," she promised. "I just need to build up to it."

She caught his smile just before he kissed her. She closed her eyes and kissed back, ignoring the catcalls and whistles that rose up around them—no doubt from her own people. She'd never live this down. But as she wrapped her arms around Duncan, she decided she could live with that.

After all, they were going to see her kissing Duncan a lot from now on.

**Thank you for reading PARADISE
(The Naravan Chronicles 4).
If you've enjoyed this book, please continue reading
for sneak peek from the next story
FLIGHT.**

CHAPTER ONE

Clare O'Malley squeezed her eyes shut and ducked her head as glass shattered against the wall near where she took cover behind an upturned table. Cursing under her breath, she fired her blaster around the edge of the barrier without looking. She didn't care if she hit anyone and her blaster was on high stun because she didn't want to actually kill anyone. But she did not want the mayhem to get any closer to her hiding spot. Getting shot in a bar brawl was not on her list of things to do tonight.

"How long are they going to keep at this?" she shouted to the man next to her as she fired into the melee again.

"Until most of them are dead," he answered with a shrug.

She glared at the cocky, spaceship captain and he flashed her a quick, sexy grin. Raf Tygran was dangerous, and not just because he was a smuggler and reputed pirate. The little tingle of interest dancing in her stomach didn't bode well for their future negotiations. But she had bigger things to worry about in that moment.

"Who the hell let t'Pree clan into a t'Kalb clan bar anyway?"

"Either someone who didn't know anything about Binneans—"

"Who doesn't know this?" she interrupted then ducked again as more glass shattered nearby. Everyone knew you couldn't put two Binnean clans in the same space. It was chemistry, science. Something to do with pheromones. You put two clans together, you got violence and mayhem. And a lot of dead Binneans plus a lot of dead and injured innocent bystanders. Humans couldn't have worked and traded with Binneans for decades without knowing this fundamental fact. *Everyone* knew putting two different clans together was disastrous.

"Or someone wanted to start a fight," Tyran finished, sending a hail of blaster fire into the chaos as a few bolts scorched the wood floor in front of their table.

"Why would anyone want to *start* a Binnean fight?"

"Got me." He ducked and put his back to the table. "But if we stay much longer, our chances of getting out in one piece go down. A lot."

"I'm ready to leave whenever you are."

He grinned again and nodded to her left. "The fighting's moving away from the front door. Stick close to the wall."

With a deep breath, she dropped the thin strap of her small purse over her head so it hung across her chest, checked the charge on her blaster, then nodded. Tygran looked around the table one last time, gauging the movements of the rolling mayhem, before moving out. They both fired randomly into the fighting as they scrambled around the edge of the room. A human man dropped back into Tygran after being punched in the face. The smuggler pushed him off and fired a few shots at the Binnean who'd thrown the punch. The giant, fur-covered being dropped to the ground stunned.

"Nice shot," Clare shouted as they continued toward the front door.

"So long as he doesn't remember it when he wakes up," Raf shouted back. "I know him."

She actually laughed. "You are in trouble."

"Wouldn't be the first time."

With a snort, she shot and stunned the two Binneans charging toward them.

"Getting a little dicey out here," she said as adrenaline roared through her blood and more than a little worry tightened her grip on her weapon.

"Then stop playing and get a move on," Raf said, sprinting toward an edge in the wall that provided some semblance of cover.

Clare followed at low run, cursing the height of her heals

and the tightness of her dress. She hadn't gotten dressed for this meeting with a blaster fight in mind.

From their new position, they were within a few meters of the front door. A handful of mostly Binneans fighting with fists and knives blocked their way.

"Now what?" she said against Raf's ear to be heard over another loud crash and the shouting.

Raf fired a few shots behind them, guarding their backs, a slight frown creasing his excessively handsome face. He took a few moments to study the fist fight blocking their exit, then grabbed her free hand and tugged. "Move!"

Resisting the urge to scream, though she doubted she'd be heard over all the other noise, Clare ran with Raf, right at the fight. As they neared, Raf fired two quick shots and Clare followed his lead by firing into the mess of bodies. The Binneans scattered, leaving the door free.

They flew out of the bar into the cool, humid air of the Docks. Still holding her hand, Raf raced down the cobbled walkway, through an alley and only slowed to a walk when they were several blocks away from the bar. Finally, he stopped and Clare took the opportunity to catch her breath.

Raf glanced down at her shoes and grinned. "You run good in those. Thought I might have to carry you."

With a crooked, cocky grin of her own, she dipped her head in thanks. "Have to be prepared in the Docks." Though, to be honest, if she'd know the night was headed in this direction, she would have chosen a lower heal.

She glanced around to get her bearings. They were smack in the middle of the city—built on the Dreic Sea and designed to look like just like the Earth city of Venice, Italy—halfway between the open sea and the bridge that crossed back to the mainland.

"Now where to?" she asked. She and Raf hadn't finished their negotiations yet. There was a deal to be made. She'd worked for months to get everything in place and she had no intention of letting a little Binnean bar brawl ruin this chance.

Raf raised his brows, then glanced down the nearest narrow alley. The beautifully built, pale stucco buildings surrounding them were fronted by elegant wrought iron or stone balconies, and just beyond the nearest building, at the end of the alleyway, she could see the black waters of one of the many canals that snaked through the Docks. The cool air was tinged with a faint hint of fish and seaweed—and a few fainter, less pleasant odors she didn't want to think about too closely.

"Come on. I know a place. Much quieter than a bar. We can finish our conversation there."

She let Raf put a hand on the small of her back to guide her, but the feel of his warm fingers against her bare back made her stomach dance dangerously. Damn him. He was doing this on purpose, to get a better deal. She knew it. He knew it. And it might have worked on another woman. But Clare was very good at negotiating.

There was a reason she had this particular dress on—

washed silk, long skirt slit up the sides to her hips, cut out back. The long sleeves and high neckline did nothing to make this dress look modest and the blue color made her pale skin glow. All of her look was very specifically designed for this meeting, to get the deal she needed to get. And she refused to waste all that effort by losing her focus just because Raf Tygran had a killer smile and was quite possibly the most handsome scoundrel she'd had the pleasure of meeting.

He led her across a small bridge, down a barely lit alley, and out into an open courtyard painted soft orange from the iron lamps spaced throughout the center of the area. The ground floors of the surrounding buildings were fronted by stone arches, hiding the actually entrances. The spaces under the arches were black this time of night, casting a sinister face on an area that would look quite charming in daylight. From beyond the courtyard, a cool breeze increased the fish and seaweed scents from the sea.

Between the breeze and the dark arches, a shiver of nerves crawled up her bare spin. She didn't want to call the sensation fear. But it was skirting close.

"Stay to the center of the courtyard," Raf warned.

"I caught the movement," she murmured. In the darkness under the arches, darker figures shuffled. Waiting for pray.

She shifted the blaster she still carried so it caught the light of a nearby lamp. The glint of metal was enough. The shadowy figures froze, or disappeared. She wasn't sure. But the threat emanating from their surroundings seemed to ease.

She noticed Tygran's blaster also shifted to plane view and smiled, wondering just how dangerous they looked to the Docks' denizens.

Raf was dressed in a sexy mix of tight black trousers, black long-sleeved shirt and a fitted, steel-colored flight jacket. But he had a kind of light, rugged handsomeness that didn't scream deadly. His blond-brown hair was short, but still brush his collar, his blue eyes sparked with mischief rather than threat. Even the way he carried himself, the confidence he exuded so effortlessly, came across as more playboy than assassin.

Yet he held his blaster like an old lover and had no trouble using it during the bar brawl. And a careful perusal had confirmed he carried at least two more concealed weapons—a knife in his calf-high boot and a second blaster at the small of his back. There was much more to Raf Tygran than was apparent at first glance. And Clare found herself…curious.

Curious was dangerous. Well, actually, the trait served her well most of the time. But when it came to men, especially those involved with a job, curiosity was potentially deadly.

As they made their way out of the courtyard and onto a walkway at the edge of the Dreic, she breathed in deeply of the murky, salty scent and forced her mind toward logical thoughts. She needed Tygran. She couldn't finish what she'd started without him. He was part of the deal. She had to keep her focus on the goal, on the negotiation and the job.

But a small part of her was still very much aware of the heat from his palm warming the bare skin along her spine.

He took another cobbled street, away from the sea and back toward the center of the city. Crossing another bridge, down a narrow alley, they came out into a small, dead-end square bracketed by tall, unadorned brick buildings. At the far side of the square was an ordinary brown door with a large brass knocker shaped like the head of an Earth camel. There weren't any other distinguishing features. Not even a series of buttons and speakers for ringing the occupants of the building.

She gave the door a dubious frown. "You know how to get in, I take it."

He grinned and swung the brass ring hanging from the camel's mouth three times without once actually hitting the door. Then he set it gently against the frame, careful not to make any noise. He stepped back and a second later the door swung open.

"Good trick," she said, trying not to laugh at his self-satisfied smirk. "If you knock the ring against the door what happens?"

"Nothing. You're ignored."

He guided her into the interior with his hand at her back again. Inside, they were greeted by dark wood, lots of dark leather and patterned rugs on hardwood floors. Smoke was thick in the air and the walls were lines with what looked to be real leather bound books. A fireplace against the far wall flickered, burning real wood. High-backed leather chairs were scattered throughout the room singly or in small clumps around inlaid tables. Men in suits from various centuries, from modern to ancient Earth, occupied most of the chairs, many of them holding cigars and brandy snifters. An androgynous looking droid in shirtsleeves and a vest manned a small bar at one corner of the room.

"Very Victorian-era Earth," she commented as Raf led her to a couple of unoccupied seats.

"Fashioned after the old men's clubs of that time period," he confirmed.

She'd noticed immediately the lack of women. "It's not an issue me being here?"

"Given most of the old farts can't take their eyes off you, I'd say no one will make a fuss."

"Well then." She returned her blaster to her little handbag and settled into a chair, crossing her legs so the entire room got a view of the full length of her thigh. "Shall we negotiate?"

Raf grinned and dropped into the seat across from her, his posture deceptively relaxed. He sprawled with his legs stretched out and crossed at the ankles, his arms draped loosely across the armrests, his blaster already returned to the shoulder harness he wore under his jacket. Yet she was sure, if needs be, that blaster would be back in his hand in the blink of an eye—maybe even faster than she'd be able to get hers from her purse even though she'd spent months practicing so she could draw quickly. The thought that he was ready for instant action was sobering. And yet his underlying current of alertness actually made her feel safer, more comfortable.

And that was even more sobering.

"Now about my fee…" he started, his eyes narrowing.

"I've offered all I'm allowed to pay," she said. "You're not getting any more."

"Ah, but you won't find another ship that can take you where you want to go. I've been there. Twice. And returned. Not another living soul can say that—outside my crew of course."

"And yet you can't get there again without the information I have. I can always give that information to another pilot. There are a lot of ships willing to take me anywhere I want to go for the fee I've named."

"Not one as good as the *Ebisu* and her crew."

She might have laughed at the boast if it wasn't true. Tygran and his crew were so notoriously good at what they did, that despite having warrants for their arrest issued on most civilized planets, they still came and went with impunity. It had taken more than a month of research to find him and arrange this meeting. And as it happened, she did need him specifically. Nathan Longfeather wouldn't help unless she could get Tygran to agree to the job. That was their deal and Longfeather was too stubborn to give her any leeway. She'd spent longer trying to get him to this point than she'd intended. She couldn't afford to lose more time.

So she needed Tygran. And he knew it, though he wouldn't know why. If he wanted more money, if he decided he wouldn't take this risk without a higher rate, she was screwed.

She stared at him while the droid from the bar brought them two snifters of Binnean brandy and set them on the small table between them. She hadn't noticed Raf ordering them, but somehow she wasn't surprised either. Even after the droid left, she took her time, sipping at her drink as she weighed her options. She had one desperate card she could play, one gambit Tygran wouldn't expect. The danger was, playing this ace could backfire.

As she let the sharp, sweet taste of the brandy slide down her throat, she decided the risk was worth it and played her card. "You're still having trouble with the Leeches. Aren't you?"

His relaxed posture stiffened subtly and his fingers tightened around his glass. He stared at her through narrowed eyes as he took another drink. Silence stretched between them, broken only by the sounds of crackling wood in the fireplace and the quiet shuffling of the other men in the room.

Raf held her gaze throughout the silence, and she didn't dare blink. She needed him to believe she'd let the Leeches know where he was, she needed him to think she'd follow through with her unspoken threat. The fact that she'd never really do that to anyone wasn't going to get her what she wanted. Fortunately, she'd been lying, and hiding her true self, for so long now, she knew he wouldn't see her bluff.

After what seemed a silent eternity, his body loosened again and a sexy grin lifted his mouth.

"Deal," he said.

She worked hard not to let him see her releasing the breath she'd been holding.

But he must have noticed because he chuckled. "Worried?"

"Maybe a little," she allowed.

"You should be. I don't like threats. Any more than I like Leeches."

"But you're still going to take the job." She made it a statement. He'd agreed. She wasn't about to let him back out now.

"I'm still taking the job." He nodded. "I'm…curious now."

That didn't bode well. "Curious?"

"You wanted me specifically for this. You're right, without the coordinates, I'm no better than any other pilot. But you were willing to threaten me to get me to agree. I find that interesting."

"You're the one who said it. You're the best. And you've been there before. And the Leeches are your weakness. I'd be a fool not to take advantage of every one of those points."

"And you're no fool, are you Clare O'Malley."

"No," she said, very seriously. "I'm no fool."

His expression turned thoughtful, considering. She didn't like that look. Raf was no fool either.

He was going to be more dangerous to her than she'd anticipated. Unlike so many of the others she dealt with, Raf lived in the underbelly and played with bad people. He was still alive, despite that. Despite the Leeches hunting him and the civilian governments on most planets after him. He was going to be a hard man to hide from, even for someone like her.

For someone whose life depended on her ability to hide, Raf Tygran was a dangerous man indeed.

**Don't miss the next romantic science fiction adventure in
The Naravan Chronicles Series
FLIGHT (The Naravan Chronicles 5)**

ABOUT THE AUTHOR

Isabo Kelly is the award-winning author of numerous science fiction, fantasy, and paranormal romances. She also writes best-selling paranormal romance under the name Kat Simons. Her life has taken her from Las Vegas to Hawaii, where she got her BA in Zoology, back to Vegas where she looked after sharks, then on to Germany and Ireland where she got her Ph.D. in Animal Behavior. Now Isabo focuses on writing. She lives in New York with her Irish husband and two beautiful boys, working as a full time writer and stay-at-home mom.

Don't miss out on new releases from Isabo! Sign up for her Newsletter here: http://eepurl.com/caxHa9

For more on Isabo and her books:
Website: http://www.isabokelly.com
Facebook: http://www.facebook.com/IsaboKelly
Twitter: https://www.twitter.com/IsaboKelly

BOOKS BY ISABO KELLY

The Naravan Chronicles

Promise

Interface

Secret

Paradise

Flight

New York Empires Anthologies

Going All In

Icing The Puck

Fire and Tears Series

Brightarrow Burning

Darkness Singed

Dawn Ignited

Fate's Hand Series

Thief's Desire

Destiny's Seduction

Kellyn's Sacrifice

The Last Guardian

Bonfire Night

For more information on Isabo's books, visit:
http://www.isabokelly.com

www.ingramcontent.com/pod-product-compliance
Lightning Source LLC
Chambersburg PA
CBHW051712180726
48283CB00004B/1321